Wings!

"Well," said the archangel, "now you have a chance to earn the rest of your feathers."

"All of them?" The little angel brushed her hands together to clean off the pepper. Then she stroked her thinly feathered wings. "All of them at once?"

"Not really at once. Our little girl, Simone, needs lots of help. For each time you help her, you'll earn a feather. She's quite a problem. I bet you'll earn your wings on this one."

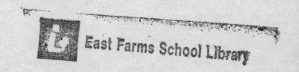

Aladdin
Angelwings
No. 2

Little Creatures

Donna Jo Napoli

illustrations by Lauren Klementz-Harte

Aladdin Paperbacks

Thank you to all my family,
and to Richard Tchen and Brenda Bowen

First Aladdin Paperbacks edition October 1999

Text copyright © 1999 by Donna Jo Napoli
Illustrations copyright © 1999 by Lauren Klementz-Harte

Aladdin Paperbacks
An imprint of Simon & Schuster Children's Division
1230 Avenue of the Americas
New York, NY 10020

Designed by Steve Scott
The text for this book was set in Minister Light and Cheltenham.
The illustrations were rendered in ink and wash.
Printed and bound in the United States of America
10 9 8 7 6 5 4 3 2 1

Library of Congress Cataloging-in-Publication Data
Napoli, Donna Jo, 1948–
Little creatures / Donna Jo Napoli ; illustrated by Lauren Klementz-Harte.
— 1st Aladdin Paperbacks ed.
p.   cm. — (Aladdin angelwings ; #2)
Summary: A little angel of Freedom hopes to earn her wings by helping
Simone understand the value of freedom, so that she will stop capturing
and imprisoning animals.
ISBN 0-689-82695-8 (pbk.)
[1. Angels—Fiction. 2. Liberty—Fiction. 3. Animals—
Treatment—Fiction.]
I. Klementz-Harte, Lauren, 1961– ill. II. Title. III. Series: Napoli,
Donna Jo, 1948– Aladdin angelwings ; #2.
PZ7.N15Li   1999   [Fic]—dc21   98-49675
CIP   AC

To my little creatures,
Elena, Mike, Nick, Eva, and Robert

Little Creatures

Angel Talk

The Little Angel of Freedom held a nectar-dipped fingertip out to the butterfly that clung to her shoulder. The butterfly sipped daintily. "Is this the house?" the little angel asked. "I don't see anyone."

"Wait," said the Archangel of Freedom. He pointed.

A girl came into the kitchen and tapped the glass jar on the table. The grasshopper inside the jar jumped. "Are you still hungry?" The girl ran out the back door and ripped a handful of grass from the yard. Then she poked the blades one by one through the holes in the jar lid. They fell soft on the grasshopper's head.

"The grasshopper needs to get out," said the Archangel of Freedom.

The little angel frowned. "The girl has made

1

sure he can breathe. And she's feeding him well." She looked at her own pet butterfly and nodded emphatically. "I think she's taking good care of him."

The girl tapped the jar again. The grasshopper jumped, but this time not so high. "Good night. Sleep tight." She ran off.

The Archangel of Freedom pointed out the window. "Yesterday, before he was caught, this grasshopper jumped from the edge of the porch up to the first crook of that peach tree." He looked at the little angel. "If you could jump that high and that far, would you be happy in a jar?"

The Little Angel of Freedom folded her hands together. She didn't look at the archangel.

A woman came into the kitchen. She picked up the jar and carried it outside. She stooped in the yard and unscrewed the lid.

The grasshopper just sat in the bottom of the jar.

The woman tilted the jar till the grasshopper slid out into the grass. He stayed there a moment, looking stunned. Then he jumped away.

"Whenever the girl catches something, the mother has to come down at night and set it free."

"Well, then, it's no problem at all," said the little angel.

"Sometimes the creature gets injured, bashing itself against the side of the jar." The Archangel of Freedom's voice was quiet and gentle. "Sometimes it even dies before the mother can set it free."

"Oh." The Little Angel of Freedom watched the grasshopper stop and chew on a leaf.

"Your wings are about halfway feathered. You've done a good job earning those feathers." The Archangel of Freedom smiled. "I'm proud of all your deeds."

"It's been hard. Every feather is so hard to earn." The little angel put her hand in her left pocket and wiggled her fingers in the ___ ___ of ground black pepper she kept there. F___ ___ was her secret tool. In her right pocket ___ kept a small pool of flower nectar for her bu___terfly. She felt fully equipped.

"Well," said the archangel, "now you have a chance to earn the rest of your feathers."

"All of them?" The little angel brushed her hands together to clean off the pepper. Then she stroked her thinly feathered wings. "All of them at once?"

"Not really at once. Our little girl, Simone, needs lots of help. For each time you help her, you'll earn a feather. She's quite a problem. I bet you'll earn your wings on this one."

Her wings. When a little angel earns her last feather, she really earns her wings, because then she can fly, like all the archangels. The little angel shivered at the thought. A bell rings when an angel earns her wings. What kind of bell would the Little Angel of Freedom hear?

The Ladybug

"Where's my grasshopper?" Simone knelt on the bench and leaned over the kitchen table propped on both elbows. Her new jeans were scratchy.

"Sit properly," said Daddy. "You're going to fall headfirst into your cereal bowl."

Simone sat on her bottom. "Where is he?"

Mamma put the milk carton in front of Simone. "I set him free. You knew I would."

"But he was mine."

"We've had this discussion before, Simone. He's better off in the yard. Eat your cereal."

Simone poured a bowl of Rice Chex. "I'm going to catch him again. And this time I'll build him a wonderful home in a shoe box. I'll fill it with real dirt and little plants . . . living plants. And he'll be just as happy as if he were outside. And I can play with him every day."

"You won't be able to see him through a shoe box," said Daddy.

"I can poke holes in the side. Viewing holes."

"No more talk about prisoner insects," said Mamma. "I don't know why you need them, anyway. We have a cat."

"The cat only comes when you feed her. Besides, I like little creatures. They can sit in my hand. They're sort of like teeny babies, but better, because they don't have to have their diapers changed. And everybody needs a baby."

"A grasshopper is like a baby? You might be the only person in the world who thinks that." Mamma took a piece of pumpernickel out of the toaster and spread jelly on it. "I'm going to the secondhand store to try to find a cheap umbrella to keep in the car for emergencies. Want to come?"

"Yay! I could use some jeans."

"Jeans? I just got you a new pair."

"I hate them. They're so stiff, I can't move right in them."

"What do you want to do?" asked Daddy. "Jump like a mother grasshopper?"

Simone laughed. She gobbled up the rest of her cereal and went outside to wait for Mamma.

A ladybug caught her eye. It crawled up a rosebush branch.

Simone moved her hand ever so slowly toward the ladybug.

Suddenly she sneezed.

Mamma came up behind her. "Are you getting a cold?"

Simone shook her head. "Do you smell pepper?"

"What? Get in the car. And, Simone, please. I saw that ladybug. I don't want you catching insects anymore."

The secondhand store was only a five-minute drive away. Mamma headed straight for the umbrellas.

Simone picked up one with penguins all over it. She waddled around. Then she spotted a funny-shaped teapot. "Look, Mamma, Aladdin's lamp." She rubbed it, but nothing came out.

They went upstairs to the women's section. Mamma tried on straw hats while Simone searched through the purses for forgotten treasures. She found a quarter, and the lady at the counter said she could keep it.

Simone and Mamma went downstairs, all the way to the basement, to the children's section.

"Would you like an elephant?" Mamma held up the stuffed blue elephant. "You could use rain boots." She held up rainbow-striped boots.

Simone headed for the jeans. But a sleeve stuck out from under the pajama bin. She pulled on it carefully. The dress was green

with three gold buttons near the neck and silver diamonds all over. The white satin collar was trimmed with lace. The material was so soft, the whole dress crushed into a ball that fit inside Simone's hands.

Without a word Mamma helped Simone put it on.

Simone twirled out of the dressing room, she twirled past Mamma paying for her dress, she twirled and twirled, all the way out to the car.

Angel Talk

"The mother told her not to catch insects anymore," said the Little Angel of Freedom. "So I guess that means I'm out of a job."

The Archangel of Freedom tilted his head. "Not so fast. Do you remember what Simone said?"

The little angel knit her brows. "I don't think she said anything when her mother told her that. But even if she didn't agree, she knows now that if she catches a grasshopper or a ladybug, her mother will get mad. So there's nothing left for me to do. But at least I earned one feather."

"You're thinking about this all wrong."

"I am?" The little angel's bottom lip quivered.

"Yes. You're making three mistakes." The

Archangel of Freedom put his hands on the little angel's shoulders. "First, it isn't enough to know her mother will scold her. Simone has to learn to respect the right for freedom all on her own, without anyone looking over her shoulder."

"Oh, yes, of course. I knew that." The little angel was annoyed at herself. Every Little Angel of Freedom knew that. "I just forgot for a moment."

The archangel smiled. "We all forget sometimes."

"That could be a hard job," said the little angel.

"And that's why I think you're going to earn a lot of feathers on this one."

The Little Angel of Freedom smiled. A lot of feathers. That's exactly what she needed. She blew a kiss to the butterfly that sat on her shoulder. "What's the second mistake I made?"

"Well, I'm sorry, but you didn't earn a feather."

"Why not? The ladybug went free."

"Simone didn't realize the ladybug needed to go free. You just distracted her for a moment."

"But that's not fair. The ladybug would be miserable now if I hadn't made Simone sneeze."

"True enough." The Archangel of Freedom nodded. "But you're not earning feathers for freeing creatures. You're earning feathers for teaching the value of freedom."

The Little Angel of Freedom thought about that. "If I get her to realize everything needs its freedom, then, naturally, she'll realize that that ladybug needed its freedom. Right?"

"Right."

"So then I can get a feather for the ladybug. Right?"

The Archangel of Freedom laughed. "Right."

The little angel smiled. "Okay, I'll get that feather later. And what's the third mistake?"

"Think back over Simone's words. If you pay careful attention to them, you'll realize that her mother didn't fully understand Simone's problem."

The little angel concentrated, but she couldn't remember anything special that Simone had said. She shrugged her shoulders in defeat.

"That's okay. Keep watching over Simone," the Archangel of Freedom said. "You'll see how she needs you."

The Tadpole

Simone heaved herself onto the couch with a sigh.

Daddy glanced at her, then went back to talking on the phone.

Simone got up and found the deck of cards. She shuffled them many times.

Daddy finished his phone call and looked at her. "What's the matter?"

"It's summer and it's not even fun."

"Go outside and play."

"There's no one to play with. Everyone's on vacation."

"That can't be true." Daddy put his hands in his pockets. "Everyone doesn't go on vacation at the same time."

"Jennifer's at Disney World. I don't want to play with anyone else. And Mamma told me I can't catch insects. The backyard was full of fireflies last night, and I couldn't catch a single one."

"Hmmm. She hasn't forbidden you to catch fish, has she?"

Simone jumped to her feet. "Fish? Can we go fishing?"

"It's Saturday, and I just put the tackle box in order yesterday. You go change out of that dress."

"But this is my new dress. And it's green. It's perfect for fishing. I bet I could even swim in it, it moves so nicely."

Daddy laughed. "All right."

Simone dashed out the kitchen door.

Simone and Daddy drove to Smedley Park. Daddy carried the poles and the tackle box. Simone carried the bucket, *thump* and *wump*, against her knees.

A turtle slipped off a log into the water. Two loons went paddling past. Frogs croaked on the small island in the pond.

Simone sat down, took off her shoes, and dipped her toes in the water. "I love fishing."

"So do I." Daddy put the bait on the hooks. Then he flung his line far out. He caught a fish almost immediately, but it was too small to eat, so he let Simone throw it back. Then he caught another one, a big one, and he swung it up onto the grass.

Simone filled the bucket with water and set it at the very edge of the grass. She took the fish off the hook and dropped it into the bucket. She swung out her own line. "Wow! I caught one, too. A giant one." But when she pulled it up, it was just a dolly stroller. "I guess I'll let it go." She carried it over to the big trash can.

After their initial luck, they got no more bites for a long time. Simone put down her pole and wandered along the edge of the water. Oh! She scooped her hands in and ran to Daddy. "Look."

The slow black tadpoles tickled her palms. "Aren't they wonderful?"

"Do you know what they are?"

"Tadpoles."

"But what are tadpoles?"

"Baby frogs, of course."

"Maybe. Or maybe baby toads. Or maybe baby newts or salamanders. It's not always easy to tell between amphibian babies."

Simone twirled. The water dripped on the front of her dress. "This is my swishy fishy dress." She laughed. "Now soggy froggy dress." She walked toward the bucket. Suddenly her nose was filled with the smell of pepper. She sneezed. Tadpoles flipped out of her shaking hands and back into the pond. She sneezed and sneezed and sneezed. Tadpoles flew through the air and plopped in the water.

All but one. Simone clutched it to her chest as she rolled on the grass sneezing. Finally she managed to get the tadpole into the bucket.

Daddy put his arm around her. "Are you all

right? I've never seen you sneeze like that before."

"I smelled pepper."

"Maybe you're developing an allergy."

"I'm okay now." Simone smiled. "And I've got my baby."

Daddy looked in the bucket. "I don't think your mother's going to be happy."

"It's not an insect." Simone looked up at Daddy earnestly. "She never said not to catch tadpoles."

Angel Talk

"She's a tricky one." The Little Angel of Freedom knit her brows.

"I told you it wouldn't be easy." The archangel touched the little angel's forehead. "If you don't succeed soon, you're going to wind up with your eyebrows permanently bunched together in worry."

The little angel giggled. She held up her hand, and her butterfly hopped from her shoulder to her finger. As she twirled around, the butterfly fluttered its wings. "I'm lucky she picked up so many tadpoles. Maybe I should get a feather for each one she dropped."

"Now who's the tricky one? Your attitude might need a little improvement."

"What do you mean?"

"Are you tempted to delay helping Simone

understand freedom so that you can earn more feathers?"

"No." The little angel's eyes opened wide. "No, I swear."

The Archangel of Freedom touched her cheek. "All right, then. Get back to work with your pepper."

"How did you know about my secret tool?"

"Archangels know a lot."

The little angel ran her fingers through the silty pepper in her pocket.

The Tub

Simone lay on her stomach on her bedroom floor and stared at the froglet in the big glass bowl. The froglet climbed onto the rock in the center and seemed to stare right back at her.

"I think he needs to go outside," said a voice from over her.

Simone rolled onto her back and looked up at Mamma. "I don't think so."

Mamma sat down on the floor. "Listen, Simone, when he was a tadpole, he might have been all right in that bowl. But now he needs to swim far and jump high. You know that."

"He's happy here. I play with him all day."

Mamma tapped the bowl with her nail. The glass made a high-pitched ringing noise. "How are you, little frog?"

The froglet blinked.

Mamma tsked and stood up. "Well, I'm going to make a nice breakfast of French toast. Get dressed." She left.

Simone put on her green dress and went toward the door. She sneezed and sneezed. She sneezed so hard, she was back on the floor rolling. She rolled right up to the froglet's bowl. The sneezes stopped. Simone lay there panting and looked at the froglet. He looked back at her.

She smiled at him.

He didn't move.

She made a crazy face.

He still didn't move.

Maybe he wasn't happy, after all.

Simone ran out of her room, through the house, and out the back door. The day was hot already, but the garage was dark and cool and damp. She grabbed a shovel and put it in the wheelbarrow. Then she rolled the wheelbarrow around to behind the garage. The ground was mossy and soft. Simone filled the wheelbarrow with dirt and weeds. She rolled it in through the back door and straight through the kitchen.

"What are you doing?" Mamma dropped the spatula on the floor.

"You'll see," sang Simone, wheeling past, down the hall, to the bathroom.

Mamma followed. "Look what a mess you're making. You're leaving dirt tracks all the way."

"I'll mop it up."

"Stop it, Simone. What on earth are you doing?"

Simone plugged the tub and dumped the dirt into it.

"George!" Mamma put her hands to her cheeks. "George!"

Daddy came running. "What?" He stared.

"It's my bathroom," said Simone. She turned on the water in the tub.

"No, young lady. It's just the bathroom you use," said Daddy.

"And you can't use it with dirt in the tub," said Mamma.

"I'll shower in your bathroom," said Simone. "Please, Mamma. I have to make Frog a nice place to play."

"Oh, honey, is that what you're up to?" Mamma looked sad. She shook her head slowly.

"Simone . . . ," began Daddy.

"Please. I want Frog to be happy. I love him. Please give me a chance. Please."

Mamma and Daddy stood with their arms around each other and watched Simone smooth out the mud on the floor of the tub.

Simone went to her room and carried Frog in his bowl to the bathroom. Frog jumped off his rock and swam in circles. Simone put the rock in the middle of the tub. Then she dumped Frog into the tub. Frog swam from one end of the tub to the other. He was fast.

Simone looked at her parents and smiled. "This is a lot better."

"In your opinion," said Mamma softly.

Angel Talk

"What a mess she's making," said the Little Angel of Freedom.

"She has a very patient mother," said the archangel.

"Right. If that mother were only a little stricter, maybe Simone would set Frog free."

The Archangel of Freedom put a hand on his hip.

"Oh, I know," said the little angel. "Simone has to learn to give up Frog on her own. I guess I was just wishing for a little more help. My pepper can only do so much."

The Archangel of Freedom smiled. "I'm glad you mentioned the pepper. Exactly how does it work?"

"I make Simone sneeze."

"Well, I figured that much. And I know that

when she caught those tadpoles, her sneezing made her drop all but one back into the water." The archangel played with the tips of his bushy sideburn. "But right now when you made her sneeze, how did the pepper help? It didn't stop her from catching anything. Yet after she sneezed she got the idea that the frog needed a better habitat."

"Sneezing is a funny thing," said the little angel. "Whenever I sneeze, it makes me stop, no matter what I am doing. It gives me a chance to think. So that's why I put it under Simone's nose. I didn't really plan to make Simone drop the tadpoles; I just wanted her to think."

"Just to think?"

"Yes. When people take the time to think, they see things differently sometimes. They act better."

The Archangel of Freedom laughed. "What a simple tool. I love it."

Leaves

Thunder boomed. Lightning zapped. Rain came in big, fat drops. Simone stood at the bathroom window with Frog by her side on the windowsill. "Oh, Frog, this is your favorite weather, isn't it?" she said.

Frog didn't say a word.

Simone sneezed. She pressed the side of her index finger against the bottom of her nose to stop more sneezes from coming. "You really should be in the rain, shouldn't you?"

Frog just stared out the window.

Simone picked up Frog and set him on his rock in the tub. Then she shut the shower curtain and reached in to turn on the cold water. The shower came down soft and steady.

Frog jumped into the water and swam like a maniac.

"See? It's better than real rain," said Simone. "It's better because it can last as long as you want." She ran to her bedroom and put on a bathing suit. Then she joined Frog in the shower.

"What's going on in here?" Mamma peeked around the shower curtain.

"Frog's happy," said Simone.

Mamma harrumphed. "Don't track mud everywhere." She turned off the shower and spread a towel on the floor. "Step out."

Simone stepped onto the towel. Her feet were muddy. "Sorry."

"It's not a good idea to take showers or a bath in a thunderstorm unless the house is grounded."

"Is our house grounded?"

"I don't really know." Mamma tapped the edge of the sink. "One foot up here."

Simone put her foot in the sink, and Mamma washed it. Then she put the other one up, and Mamma washed it.

"Simone, honey, I'm trying to be as understanding as I can be. But this mud gets to me. It's just so . . . I don't know, so muddy. I don't want mud in the house."

"Frog needs it."

"Well, I need a clean house. You can't keep this up."

Simone looked at Mamma. "I don't know what else to do." Her voice quavered.

"You have to figure something out. Soon."

Simone nodded. Then she ran to her bedroom.

In the morning the sun came out.

"Where's my green dress?" called Simone.

"It's in the wash."

Simone ran to the closet and took out her purple dress. Then she ran to the bathroom and opened the shower curtain.

Frog blinked at her.

Simone sneezed. She pressed her finger hard against the underside of her nose.

33

"Okay, okay, so you need to go outside. We can take a walk together." She picked up Frog, and they went out the door.

Broken branches and leaves were strewn across the yard. Simone ran inside and found her green yarn. Then she went back outside and put Frog on the ground. He hopped and blinked and hopped.

Simone poked holes with a stick in the big, flat leaves. She overlapped them in a fan shape and ran the yarn through. "A big, leafy hat for me." She put it on her head. She picked up smaller leaves and set to work. "A small, leafy hat for you." She put it on Frog's head.

Frog jumped, and his hat flew off.

Simone laughed.

Angel Talk

O h, poor Simone. She's got to come up with another plan for Frog fast. Her mother wants the tub clean." The Little Angel of Freedom tugged on the archangel's sleeve. "Can you think of something? I'll whisper it to her in her sleep, if only we can come up with a solution."

"Weren't you the one who wanted her mother to be stricter so that she'd set Frog free faster?"

"That was before. They take showers together now. They're real friends," said the little angel. "They wear leafy hats together. What more could you want?"

"Freedom," said the archangel. "That's what we're all about, after all."

The little angel put her finger in front of her

butterfly, and it hopped on. She looked at it thoughtfully. Then she looked at the archangel. He was watching her, and there was something in the archangel's eyes that made the little angel feel worried, just the slightest bit.

The Snake

Frog hopped across the yard and into the empty lot next door.

Simone followed.

Frog slopped through a puddle as wide as a muddy sea.

"Happy hopper," said Simone, slopping merrily behind. Then she stopped.

A thin, greenish-brown body curled along in the tall, wet grasses. A snake. And it had its eye on Frog.

Simone's hand itched to grab that snake tail. She hadn't caught a snake in almost a year. Then she sneezed.

She looked around. Frog was gone. The snake was gone. Simone ran through the puddle. "Frog, Frog, where are you?"

Frog jumped over her shoe.

"Oh, Frog. I'm so glad you're safe." Simone picked up Frog and sat down on a log to hold him close. "Look." The two of them watched the snake glide away. "See? You're much safer if you stay with me."

Frog blinked.

"I can't keep you in the tub anymore. Mamma can't stand it. So it's back to your glass bowl. But I'll take you on walks every day, and I'll always keep you safe."

Angel Talk

J ust look," said the Little Angel of Freedom. "Now she's got a good reason to keep the frog prisoner."

"What reason?" asked the Archangel of Freedom.

"He's safer with her. It's true. The world is full of things that eat frogs. Even some people eat frogs."

The archangel pushed the little angel's hair back from her face and looked steadily at her. "Is it safe to cross the street?"

"What? You mean for you and me?"

"No, I mean for people."

The Little Angel of Freedom smiled in confusion. "Well, if they look both ways and cross at the corner."

"Always? Is it always perfectly safe if

you're careful and cross only at the corner?"

The little angel thought of all sorts of awful accidents. "Not always."

"Hmmm. I guess that means Simone would be safer if we locked her up in a bathroom."

The little angel gulped.

"Maybe her parents need to be protected, too," said the Archangel of Freedom. "We could lock them up. In fact, maybe everyone . . ."

"Okay, okay," said the little angel. "We can't lock up the whole world."

"See?"

The little angel took the archangel's hand. "You're right. That frog has to go free."

Twins

Mamma pushed the cart down the frozen foods aisle. She loaded up on orange juice. Simone chose toaster waffles. She couldn't wait to eat them.

That was everything; the cart was full. Mamma got into line.

"Look." Simone pointed at the ring machine.

"Those rings turn your fingers green. Remember?"

Green fingers. Like Frog's fingers. "I'll be twins with Frog. Please. I need a quarter."

"Okay. We'll take it out of your allowance." Mamma looked in her purse. "All I have is a dime and three nickels."

"Oh, I forgot." Simone reached into her own pocket. There was the quarter she'd found in the used clothing store. She stood in front of the glass globe full of rings. They had gems in all colors. Simone put her quarter in place. She squeezed her eyes shut and wished. Then she turned the little handle.

Plink.

An emerald. Perfect.

All the next week, Simone wore her emerald. She moved it often from finger to finger, until all ten fingers had a green line around the bottom.

Then she carried Frog into the kitchen while Mamma was cooking dinner.

"This is my twin, Frog." She held up her green fingers.

"Your twin? You're not twins."

"Twins forever."

Mamma gave a crooked smile. "Look at your feet."

"Frog has toes. Me, too."

"Look at your head."

"Frog has eyes. Me, too."

"Hmmm. Stir this for me, would you?" Mamma went out the back door.

Simone stirred happily while Frog hopped around on the table.

Mamma came back in. She held her hands cupped together so that Simone couldn't see what was inside. She put them close to Frog and opened her fingers just a little. A cricket jumped out.

Frog blinked. He shot out his tongue and ate the cricket.

"There's one more in my hands." Mamma looked at Simone. "Are you hungry?"

Simone laughed. "This is my friend, Frog. Friends forever."

Mamma laughed, too. "How do you do, Frog? Nice to meet you. Would you like another cricket?"

She opened her hands, and Frog ate the cricket.

Angel Talk

I'm never going to get anywhere if that mother's going to make it so much fun to keep the frog." The Little Angel of Freedom paced before the archangel. "She used to be on our side."

"Oh, I think she's still on our side. Didn't you notice how she sang as she washed the mud out of the tub?"

"That's only because she was happy to have a clean bathroom again. She doesn't seem to care about the frog being a prisoner anymore. Whoever heard of a mother who catches crickets? Her skin should crawl at the very idea. That's how adult women are."

"Remember, this mother has had years of experience freeing insects," said the Archangel of Freedom. "I doubt much makes her skin crawl."

"But she should have been upset that the frog ate the poor crickets."

"Really? And what's the poor frog supposed to eat? Toast with jelly?"

The little angel shook her hands in frustration. "Of course not. And she's allowed Simone to catch insects to feed the frog all along, I know that. But, somehow, it just seems like she's turned on us. She's joining Simone."

"Maybe not. Maybe she's just not fighting her anymore." The archangel hooked his arm through the little angel's arm. "You and I both know Simone has to free that frog on her own. Maybe this mother knows that, too." He patted the little angel's hand. "Anyway, it doesn't really matter what anyone else thinks right now. The task of helping Simone is yours."

"The frog's become very important," said the little angel slowly. "Simone really loves him. She loves him, and she'll have to give him up. That's so sad."

"Is that a new butterfly on your shoulder?"

The little angel perked up. "Oh, I have new butterflies all the time. Butterflies only live a short while. So when I find one coming out of its cocoon, I quickly put it on my shoulder and feed it nectar so it won't fly away. It lives happily on my shoulder for its whole life."

"Why don't you want it to fly away?"

"Butterflies are beautiful."

"If it flew away, what would it do?"

"Sip nectar from flowers," said the little angel.

"Is that all?"

No, thought the little angel. It would have a chance to fly all over the skies. All the angels could share its beauty. But she didn't say that. She couldn't speak for the sadness in her throat.

Hair Spray
and Candy

Daddy looked at the list again. "Where would the shampoo be?"

"Don't act dumb, Daddy." Simone giggled and pointed to the sign at the front of aisle 4. It said SHAMPOO in big letters. "You always act like you don't know anything when Mamma sends us to the drugstore."

"I hate shopping."

"I love it." Simone twirled in a circle around Daddy. "And I love this dress. It makes me want to dance all the time."

"Hmmm. Haven't I seen that dress before?" asked Daddy.

Simone giggled again. "I wear it every day. Unless Mamma hides it. Or steals it to wash."

"It's a nice dress." Daddy wandered slowly over to aisle 4. "What kind should I buy?"

"You mean Mamma didn't write down the brand?"

"No. It says here, 'Shampoo for normal hair—cheapest.'" Daddy peered closely at the price labels under the bottles of shampoo. "Help me."

Simone reached for a bottle and handed it to Daddy.

"How'd you do that so fast?"

"The store brand is always cheapest," said Simone.

Daddy nodded. "Of course. You just saved me a lot of time with the rest of this list, Simone. How about I buy you one treat for helping me out."

"Great." Simone's eyes strayed down the aisle. She walked over and picked up a can. Hair spray. Green hair spray. She dropped it in the plastic basket on Daddy's arm.

"What's this?"

"My treat."

They finished their shopping and stood in line. Simone and Daddy both looked over the candies.

"You already got a treat," said Daddy.

"I didn't ask for another," said Simone. She picked up a bag of green spearmint leaves, then put them down again. She looked sideways at Daddy—he loved spearmint leaves as much as she did.

Daddy laughed and put the spearmint leaves in his basket. Yum.

When they got home, Simone took the bag of candy and the can of hair spray and went right to her bedroom. "Croak, Froggy. Croak croak."

Frog sat in his glass bowl and looked at her.

Simone read the directions on the side of the can. "Daddy, come help me," she called.

Daddy opened the door slightly. "What's up?"

"Come on in. Here." Simone handed him the can. "Spray my hair."

Daddy read the can. "Green?"

"Yup."

"Hmmm. Mamma told me you were trying to become Frog's twin, but this is going too far."

"I'm not going to be a frog," said Simone. "I'm going to be a witch. A green witch. And Frog will be my toad."

"It's not Halloween."

"Who cares? Spray me. Please."

"What if you don't like having green hair?"

Simone jumped up and down. "Read the can. The other side. It says the color washes out with ordinary shampoo."

Daddy read the other side of the can. "Okay. You got me."

"Yay." Simone put her hands over her face and turned slowly as Daddy sprayed.

"All done." Daddy put the can on her bureau.

Simone looked at the backs of her hands. They were green. She looked in her mirror. Her hair was bright green. "Abracadabra," she screamed. "You're a newt, Daddy."

Daddy jumped back. "I am?" He slunk away.

Simone did a little witch dance in front of the window. Then she opened the bag of spearmint leaves. "Hey, Newt-Daddy," she called. "Want a candy?" She ran down the hall and gave Daddy a candy.

Back in her room, she sat on her bed with Frog on her lap. She chewed on a spearmint leaf and scraped off little pieces from another one with her nails. Then she used her spit to stick the pieces together. She put her creation on her palm and held it in front of Frog. "See? This is our magic green fly."

Frog zapped it with his tongue. It disappeared down his throat.

"Oh!" Simone laughed. "Did you like that? I'll make another." She sneezed. And sneezed and sneezed and sneezed. She sneezed till her eyes ran. When she finally stopped, she looked at Frog. "Maybe one candy fly is enough."

Frog blinked.

Angel Talk

You shouldn't have let her feed the frog that candy."

"I didn't let her," said the little angel, wringing her hands. "I had no idea she was going to do it. Probably she had no idea. It was the frog's idea. I made her sneeze as soon as I realized what was happening."

The Archangel of Freedom pulled the little angel close. "Poor silly little frog."

"Will he get sick?"

"I don't know."

"Oh, what should I do?" The Little Angel of Freedom put her arms across her chest and hugged herself. "Oh, no."

"Keep watch," said the archangel. "That's all you can do, now."

Ice-Pops

Simone heard the front door close. She ran to greet Mamma.

"Yikes!" Mamma stared. "Is that you?"

"I'm a witch."

"You can say that again. How'd you make your hair green?"

"I bought hair spray. Daddy helped me."

"George," called Mamma.

No one answered.

"Maybe he's hiding," said Simone.

"He better be." Mamma went into the living room and sank into the cushions on the couch.

"How'd your night class go?"

"Okay. I have a lot of homework." Mamma leaned back. She patted the cushion beside her. "Come cuddle with me, my little green child."

Simone snuggled up to Mamma.

"Green dress, green fingers, and now green hair. And, oh my, the backs of your hands are green." Mamma leaned away so that she could look Simone in the face. "Maybe you really are turning into a frog."

Simone took a spearmint leaf from her pocket and offered it to Mamma.

Mamma popped it in her mouth. "I love these."

"Everyone does. Even Frog."

"What do you mean, even Frog?"

"I made a green fly out of one, and Frog ate it."

Mamma sat up straight. "Frog ate candy?"

"He liked it."

Mamma went quickly to Simone's bedroom, with Simone at her heels. "Frog, are you okay?"

Frog sat in his bowl with his eyes closed.

"Oh, no," said Simone. "Is he sick?"

"Maybe." Mamma touched Frog lightly on his back.

Frog opened his eyes. Then he shut them again.

"Does he ever act this way?" asked Mamma.

"Never. Oh, Mamma. What should we do?"

"Take him out just a minute."

Simone held Frog while Mamma lined the bottom of the bowl with a wet washcloth. Then she gently put him back in place.

Frog didn't even open his eyes.

"Is he dying?" Simone's voice cracked.

"Well, he's still sitting up. That's a good sign. Let's let him rest now. Come with me."

Simone followed Mamma into the kitchen.

"You could use a little picker-upper," said Mamma. "I bought a box of ice-pops this morning."

"I don't really feel like an ice-pop right now." Simone slumped into a chair.

Mamma opened the freezer. "Lime—your favorite." She held out an ice-pop. "It doesn't do anyone good to sit and worry. There's nothing we can do now but hope. So let's go in the backyard and eat ice-pops and watch the fireflies."

Frog would love to watch fireflies if he felt well, thought Simone. And he'd love to eat them. But she didn't say a word.

Angel Talk

The Little Angel of Freedom sat with her knees pulled up to her chest and her head tucked down. She rocked from side to side.

The Archangel of Freedom sat beside her, cross-legged.

"Aren't you going to tell me that being safe in Simone's home wasn't safe at all? That everything's a risk. Aren't you going to say that?" asked the little angel, not looking up.

The archangel didn't say a word.

The little angel was silent, too, for a long, long while. "Aren't you going to tell me that I shouldn't fret now? That what's done is done. That all I can do is keep watch. Like you said before. Aren't you going to say it again?"

The archangel didn't say a word.

Finally the little angel lifted her head. She moved closer to the archangel and snuggled under his wing.

Morning

Simone woke with the dawn. She was on her side, facing the wall. "Please be alive," she said. "Please, please. But if you're dead, Frog," she whispered, "if you're dead, I'm sorry. I'm so, so sorry." Her eyes filled with tears. She rolled over.

Frog sat in the bowl and blinked at her. Beside him was a pile of very green droppings.

"Yay!" shouted Simone.

Mamma and Daddy came in.

"He's alive," said Daddy.

"Thank heavens," said Mamma.

"Want to take the day off from work, Daddy? We can go fishing."

Daddy frowned. "Well, Frog's being alive is worth a celebration, but I don't know about missing work."

"I have to go back to the pond."

"Why?"

Simone licked her lips. She looked long at Frog. Then she turned to her parents decisively. "Frog's going home today."

Mamma kissed Simone on the cheek. "I think I'll drive Daddy to work today, so he doesn't have to take the train. And on the way we can pass by the pond together, all three of us with Frog."

"Let me get my dress on. It's what I was wearing when I first found Frog. And it's what I want him to remember me in."

Mamma and Daddy and Simone drove to the park. Simone sat in the back with the glass bowl on her lap. She held Frog in her hands inside the bowl, but Mamma insisted on bringing the bowl so that Frog couldn't hop out in the car.

Then they walked down the path to the pond's edge.

"Good-bye, Frog." Simone put the bowl on

the ground. She reached in to take out Frog, but at that very moment Frog took a giant leap, right out the bowl and over Simone's shoulder.

Simone fell backward onto her bottom. Her legs shot out, and the bowl tumbled against a rock and cracked apart with a loud ring.

Frog sat beside Simone and blinked. Then he splashed into the pond and disappeared.

"Friends forever," said Simone, brushing the dirt off her dress. "Above water and below. Friends forever."

"He'll be happy now," said Mamma. She picked up the pieces of the bowl.

"He'll have the right things to eat," said Daddy.

"You don't have to try to make me feel better," said Simone. "I know. I'm okay."

Angel Thoughts

The newest Archangel of Freedom blew on her inside-out pocket. She had rinsed out the nectar earlier, but the pocket was still wet. Oh, well. It didn't matter. It would dry as she flew. She grinned at the idea.

"Lead the way," she said to the butterfly on her shoulder.

The butterfly waited for nectar.

"There's no more nectar coming from me," said the angel. "You have to go exploring among the flowers. It'll be fun. You'll see."

The butterfly flew off.

The angel spread her wings. They were full. Now she was truly glad at how many tadpoles Simone had caught on that fishing day. When Simone brought Frog back to the pond, the

angel's wings had suddenly grown thick with feathers.

And the ring of the cracking bowl was the bell sound that the angel had been waiting for. She smiled. It wasn't exactly an elegant bell, but she liked it because now no other creature would ever be trapped in that bowl. She had earned these wings.

The newest Archangel of Freedom swooped in and out of the flowers, right behind the butterfly. After all, what could be better than flying free with a friend?

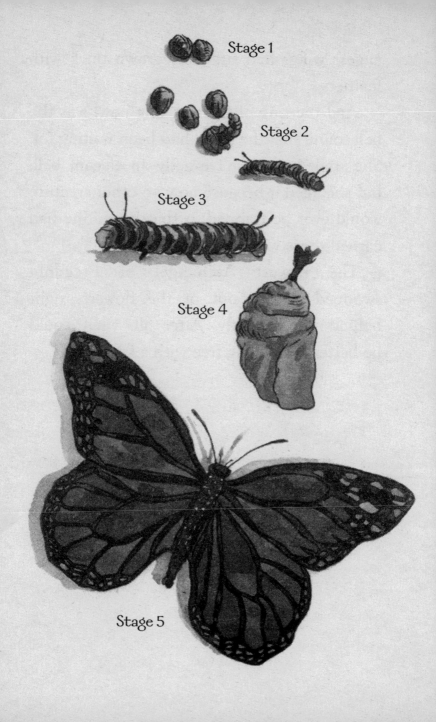

Stage 1

Stage 2

Stage 3

Stage 4

Stage 5

Life Cycle of a Butterfly

1 Egg stage: the mother lays eggs on or near a plant

2 Larva stage: the egg hatches and out comes a caterpillar

3 Pupa stage: the caterpillar grows and grows

4 Cocoon (or Chrysalis) stage: the caterpillar wraps itself in a silk cocoon

5 Adult stage: a fully grown butterfly is born

Meet the Little Angel of Independence
in the next ***Angelwings***

No. 3 On Her Own

I have the perfect task for you, little angel," said the Archangel of Independence. "Are you ready to come?"

The Little Angel of Independence looked down at the archangel from his perch in the tree house. He had been expecting to be given another task soon. He loved helping children. And he was looking forward to hearing the bell that would ring when he earned his wings. That couldn't be very far off—he almost had all his feathers already. Still, he didn't like the way the archangel asked that question. His chest tightened. "In the past I've done all my tasks with a little angel partner. Can't I have a partner this time?"

"You won't need one. The problem is obvious."

"To you," said the little angel. "But it might not be so obvious to me."

The Archangel of Independence smiled. "This is a task for you—not for any other little angel. But I'll be by your side as long as you need me."

The little angel waved good-bye to his friends and climbed down the ladder. He took the archangel's hand.

Off they went to a schoolroom. The little angel stayed very close to the archangel as he looked around. Both of them were invisible to the children. Still, they held back in a corner, out of the way.

The children sat at their desks coloring the fronts of large manila envelopes. Sweat beads formed across their brows, despite the open windows. One boy stopped for a moment and gazed out at the empty playground. A girl scratched her ankle, then got absorbed in readjusting the straps on her new sandals. Other than that, the class was busy.

"They look pretty normal to me," said the Little Angel of Independence. "No one's nagging the teacher for extra directions or copying a friend's artwork or anything else that shows a weak spirit. How can I tell who's lacking independence?"

The Archangel of Independence stood beside him, attentive and quiet, as though he hadn't heard a word the little angel said.

The little angel yanked on the archangel's hand, which he still held tight. "Whom should I help?"

"Try to figure it out," said the Archangel of Independence.

The teacher rapped his desk with his knuckles. "Okay, everyone. Now take the loose papers from your desks and slide them into your envelopes. I'm going to pass back your last few quizzes for you to put in, too." He got up and walked down the aisles handing back sheets of paper. "Be sure to show them to your parents."

The children obediently lifted their desk lids and stuffed their envelopes. One boy checked to see what his neighbor was doing.

The Little Angel of Independence moved closer to the boy, pulling the archangel with him. "Is it he?"

The boy's hand darted into his neighbor's desk and emerged with a small plastic bag. "These are my water balloons. I knew you stole them," he hissed.

The other little boy twisted his mouth to one side. "I was going to give them back. I just forgot."

"Yeah, sure."

"I was. Today, in fact. Since it's the last day of school. I was going to do it today."

The little angel turned away. Stealing was a problem, all right. But that's not the problem he had been chosen to deal with. He looked around the room one more time.

The teacher walked the aisles, holding the trash can. "Put your math books on the back table and your reading books on the shelf by the windows. Then dump anything you want to get rid of into this can."

Two girls got up and hooked arms as they carried their math books to the back table. They looked pretty dependent on each other.

The Little Angel of Independence pulled the archangel with him as he followed the girls.

But then one of them skipped back to her desk, and the other one stayed to neaten up the book stacks as the other children dropped off their math books.

"It's not one of them." The Little Angel of Independence sighed. "Who is it?"

The Archangel of Independence remained silent.

A buzzer went off.

"That's it, kids. The school year is over." The teacher half-sat on the edge of his desk and smiled. "Have a great summer."

Happy conversation broke out all over the room as the children gathered their things and went out the door.

The angels followed them outside.

One little girl with ribbons in her braids had stopped in the middle of the sidewalk to fiddle with her backpack.

"Hey, Elena," called another girl as she passed by, "want to go to the ice-cream store?

My mom gave me and my big sister money to celebrate the last day of school."

Elena reached inside her backpack and pulled out a stuffed giraffe. Its matted fur was totally worn off in places, and its neck flopped to one side. "I can't. Kathy doesn't feel like going out, and I've got to take care of her." She kissed the giraffe and tucked it under her arm.

The other girl got on the bus and tapped the shoulder of the girl beside her. She pointed at Elena through the bus window. They both laughed.

Elena slung her backpack over one shoulder and ran for home.

"That's the one I'm supposed to help?" asked the little angel.

The Archangel of Independence nodded. "I knew you'd discover her on your own."

Don't miss these other
Aladdin *Angelwings* stories:

No. 1
Friends Everywhere

No. 3
On Her Own

No. 4
One Leap Forward

Earn Your Wings!
essay contest

Win

✱ A $250 Gap gift certificate

✱ Your name in an Aladdin Angelwings book

✱ $100 worth of Simon & Schuster
Children's books

✱ $250 worth of Simon & Schuster Children's
books donated to your school's library

✱   ✱   ✱

Describe your good deed in
300 words or less for your
chance to win.

Have you earned your
Angelwings?

Official Rules
Aladdin Angelwings
"Earn Your Wings" Contest

1. No purchase necessary. Submission must include one original essay on the good deed you have done (not to exceed 300 words). Entries should be typed (preferable) or printed legibly. Mail your essay to: Simon & Schuster Children's Publishing Division, Marketing Department, Aladdin Angelwings "Earn Your Wings" Contest, 1230 Avenue of the Americas, New York, New York 10020. Each essay can only be entered once. Contest begins September 15, 1999. Entries must be received by December 31, 1999. Not responsible for postage due, late, lost, stolen, damaged, incomplete, not delivered, mutilated, illegible, or misdirected entries, or for typographical errors in the rules. Entries are void if they are in whole or in part illegible, incomplete, or damaged. Enter as often as you wish, but each entry must be different and mailed separately. Essays will be judged by Simon & Schuster Children's Publishing on the following basis: 80% good deed done, 20% writing ability. All entries must be original and the sole property of the entrant. Entries must not have been previously published or have won any awards. All submissions become the property of Simon & Schuster and will not be returned. By entering, entrants agree to abide by these rules. Void where prohibited by law.

2. Winner will be selected from a judging of all eligible entries received and will be announced on or about March 1, 2000. Selected entrant will be notified by mail.

3. One Consumer Grand Prize: The winner will receive a $250 gift certificate at Gap Clothing Stores, $100 worth of Simon & Schuster Children's Publishing books, have $250 worth of Simon & Schuster Children's Publishing books donated to his or her school's library, and have his or her name appear in a future Aladdin Angelwings book. The winner's essay may appear in future publication(s) from Simon & Schuster or advertising for the Aladdin Angelwings series.

4. Contest is open to legal residents of U.S. and Canada (excluding Quebec). Winner must be 14 years of age or younger as of December 31, 1999. Employees and immediate family members (or those with which they are domiciled) of Simon & Schuster, its parent, subsidiaries, divisions, and related companies and their respective agencies and agents are ineligible. Prize will be awarded to the winner's parent or legal guardian.

5. Prize is not transferable and may not be substituted except by Simon & Schuster. In the event of prize unavailability, a prize of equal or greater value will be awarded.

6. All expenses on receipt of prize, including federal, state, provincial and local taxes, are the sole responsibility of the winner. Winner's legal guardian will be required to execute and return an Affidavit of Eligibility and Release and all other legal documents that Simon & Schuster may require (including but not limited to an assignment to Simon & Schuster of all rights including copyright in and to the winning essay and the exclusive right of Simon & Schuster to publish the winning entry in any form or media) within 15 days of attempted notification or an alternate winner will be selected.